Raps, Chants, and Rants

by

Nadja

NadjaMedia.com

NadjaMedia.com

Nadja Media
530 Los Angeles Ave., Suite 115
Moorpark, California 93021

ISBN -- 10: 1-942057-15-6
ISBN – 13: 978-1-942057-15-4

Dedication

This work is dedicated to Humanity
at this most exciting Time of Transformation
of ourselves and of our Planet.

Acknowledgments

Thank you to Source Energy and Mother Nature
for supporting our lives and our dreams.

Foreword

The selections in this book were created to inspire us at this Time of Great Change to grow into the best version of ourselves. Basically they are short messages of hope and encouragement. It is a companion version to the MP3/CD Raps, Chants, and Rants spoken word album. The lyrics open our hearts and fill us with excitement about the possibilities of the period of history we are now living through. The art consists of codes that carry helpful energies similar to the raps. Gaze upon them with an open heart and a quiet mind.

In spite of appearances we are currently moving toward a magnificent future. The best is yet to come. The Light *will* be victorious. Keep the faith.

Chants

To create chants from this work, a leader will say the first two lines and then the audience will repeat them. Then the leader says the next two lines and then the audience repeats these. Continue this for each entire piece. This will help embed the words into the consciousness of those repeating them.

Contents

Callin' in the Tribe

Now is the time

Of the Dreamers and the Doers

Now is the time

For the Shakers and the Movers

Now is the time

To saddle it up

Giddy up, giddy up

Giddy up, giddy up

Callin' in the Tribe

We can fly high

And we can fly low

We can heal the Earth

As we go

We came to Earth

Just to do all this

Come on now

Let's live our bliss

Callin' in the Tribe

Hey out there

I'm callin' in the Tribe

We are here

And we are alive

Now is the time

Of the Dreamers and the Doers

Now is the time

For the Shakers and the Movers

Callin' in the Tribe

Now is the time

To saddle it up

Giddy up, giddy up

Giddy up, giddy up

Over the Globe

We're billions strong

Come on now

Just come on along

Callin' in the Tribe

Hey out there

Are you one?

Come with us

And join the fun

Look in the mirror

See who you are

Oh, my, yes

We've come so far

Callin' in the Tribe

Now is the time

Of the Dreamers and the Doers

Now is the time

For the Shakers and the Movers

Now is the time

To saddle it up

Giddy up, giddy up

Giddy up, giddy up

Conduit

Plug into the Circuit

Be a conduit

Running the energy

Running the energy

Directing it out

To where it needs to be

To awaken every particle

To wake up you and me

That's right

That's right

Bring in the Light

Bring in the Light

Conduit

Open up your portals

And bring in the Light

That's right

That's right

A radiant cell tower

Filled with the Light

Just plug into the Energy

Its majesty and might

That's right

That's right

Step it up

Step it up

Conduit

Working with the Light

Working with the Light

To bring the world to balance

And make everything right

Yes, make everything right

To bring the world to balance

And make everything right

That's right

That's right

Help bring the world to balance

By radiating Light

Help bring the world to balance

By radiating Light

The Golden Pyramid Song

(cosmicdisclosure.com)

The Golden Pyramid

Said to me

Get these words out

And you'll soon see

They'll help bring on all the changes

That are meant to be

They'll help bring on all the changes

That are meant to be

They'll help bring on all the changes

That are meant to be

The Golden Pyramid Song

I forgive you

Do you forgive me?

So we can go forward

In true unity

Do you love you?

I love me

As we practice this

We set ourselves free

The Golden Pyramid Song

Do you forgive you?

I forgive me

This is part of the plan

To just Be and let Be

If we do all this

We will all soon see

How we can change our world

And set everyone free

Evolution Revolution

Look up and live

A revolution's going on

It's spreading everywhere

Come along and sing your song

We are all changing

We are growing and evolving

There's a worldwide revolution

You are needed for resolving

Evolution Revolution

The Planet's in trouble

Your help is needed badly

The situation's very serious

And it might end sadly

The greatest revolution

Is right inside of you

Daily count your blessings

And your mind will renew

Evolution Revolution

Nothing to be thankful for?

What about the sky

The stars, the sun

And the birds that fly by?

The flowers, the trees

Your body, the Earth

The chance to laugh and cry

Since the day of your birth?

Evolution Revolution

There's a revolution

Look up and live

Say Yes to life

Find out what you can give

We have no time to waste

You came to play your part

Your help is badly needed

Learn to live from your heart

Evolution Revolution

Don't entertain the negative

The ugly and the Dark

These thoughts stop you

From playing your true part

Your life may be hard

Filled with sadness and pain

But by daily counting blessings

You have everything to gain

Evolution Revolution

You can crawl out

From that deeply hidden cave

Where it's dark, cold, and lonely

Seek the Light and be brave

Hurt grows anger

Anger grows hate

This can mess up your life

And darken your fate

Evolution Revolution

Listen to your anger

Let it talk to you

Find out where it comes from

Release and renew

Watch what you're thinking

Don't believe your mind

It's the Big Trickster

And will keep you blind

Evolution Revolution

What is your talent?

You were born with one or more

Seek it out, develop it

Then you will score

You are worthy

You are loved

This is the Gift

Given from Above

Evolution Revolution

Get really quiet

Away from friends and noise

In gratitude and praise

Listen for the Voice

You may not hear it

On your first try

But do this daily

And someday by and by

Evolution Revolution

You will hear that small voice

From down deep within

It will guide you truly

Through the thick and the thin

You will learn how to love

Yourself and others

The world all around you

Your sisters and your brothers

Evolution Revolution

Don'tcha know

We are all One

The world and its people

Mother Nature and the Sun

Let go of the past

It is dead

Live moment to moment

In the Light instead

Evolution Revolution

Be happy, find joy

Welcome each day

Greet everyone you see

This is the way

Don't be a follower

Think for yourself

Go deep within

Find the True Wealth

Evolution Revolution

Be the change

You would like to see

To heal Mother Earth

Every person and tree

Come out of the shadows

Live in the Light

Play your true part

Both day and night

Evolution Revolution

Look deep within

Surrender, let go

Let the Light in

Go with Its flow

We have no time to waste

You came to play your part

Your help is needed badly

Learn to live from your heart

Evolution Revolution

Look up and live

A revolution's going on

It's spreading everywhere

Come along and sing your song

Age of Aquarius

The Age of Aquarius

Has now begun

Open up to peace

Bury your gun

It's gonna be

A wild ride

As you rewire yourself

From deep down inside

Activate your heart

To really see

Drop all your barriers

So you can just Be

Age of Aquarius

The Age of Aquarius

Is finally here

We can love one another

Without any fear

No more war

Not any more

We'll be safe

Not like before

Love yourself

Love each other

Wake up World

We're all sisters and brothers

Age of Aquarius

The Age of Aquarius

Is finally here

We can leave our trenches

Without any fear

Yes, we're brothers and sisters

All over the globe

Take a deep breath

And watch it all unfold

Think Paint

Think paint

Think paint

What I am

And what I ain't

What I think

I create

Hey, wait

Time out for me to cogitate

That means

No one's to blame

For what I make

But me...

Think Paint

Whoa…

So now let's see

How I can change

My reality

Switch my thoughts

Switch my life

No more nightmare

No more strife

Create the best world

I know how

What a game

It's fun to play

Think Paint

I now know how

To create my day

Use my mind

As an artist's tool

Tell it what

I want it to do

To paint my world

With colors bright

That vibrate with

The highest Light

What a paintbrush

What a tool

Think Paint

It's absolutely

Very cool

Hey, we're all artists

Whoever knew!

Try it, Try it

Be my guest

Stick with the program

Create the life

That suits you best

Come join the fun

And you'll soon see

How to create your reality

Think Paint

Think Paint

Think Paint

What I am

And what I ain't

What I think

I create

No one's to blame

For what I make

But me

Now I see

Switch my thoughts

Switch my life

No more nightmare

No more strife

Ship of Light

I'm speedin' on the fast track

Burn karma burn

And don't come back

I ain't gonna do

No more harm

I am gonna

Completely disarm

Lay down my mask

Nothin' to hide

I'm now totally clean

And fresh inside

Let the energy flow

Ship of Light

Go, Baby, go

I'm gonna climb up on

A Ship of Light

I swear I'm gonna

Do it right

I'm not completely healed yet

But what you see

Is what you get

After all, I'm only human

What the heck

Climb aboard

There's room for you

Ship of Light

You can grow

And heal, too

Yep, I'm speedin' on the fast track

I'm burnin' my karma

And I ain't gonna

Get it back

Watch out!

I'm barreling down the rail

OMG and Holy Grail

I'm laughin' inside

It's a hot, wild ride

Oh, Go Daddy

Ship of Light

Hold on Paddy

Let the energy run

The fun's begun

Come on aboard

The Ship of Light

Get your act together

The future's bright

Outta the Box

Are you wanting

To get out of the box?

Every day

Opportunity knocks

Do you fear

To take the leap

Into the unknown?

Is the risk too steep?

Outta the box

Outta the box

Energy rocks

And opportunity knocks

Outta the Box

Hey, Hey

Wouldn't you love

To set yourself free?

Be all of what

You were born to be?

Liberate yourself

Outta the box

Outta the box

Energy rocks

And opportunity knocks

Oh Yeah

Find out

Outta the Box

What you're made of

Give this a try

It's always helpful

To question why

Is your life

Working for you?

Are you doing

What you really want to do?

Outta the box

Outta the box

Opportunity knocks

And energy rocks

Outta the Box

Many are doing this

Now is the time

To take your life in your hands

And rise and shine

Hey, Hey

Liberate yourself

Outta the box

Outta the box

Outta the box

Energy rocks

And opportunity knocks

Outta the box

Outta the Box

Outta the box

Outta the box

Oh yeah

Outta the box

54

All Aboard The Glory Train

Are you up?

Are you awake?

Let's get goin'

Take off the brake

Get on up

And move on out

Strut your stuff

And give a shout

Cause we are on

The Glory Train

Goin' straight up

To the top

All Aboard The Glory Train

At full speed

And we won't stop

Woo Hoo

Chugga, Chugga

Boom, Boom

Flash

Come on now

The past is past

Forget about the media

Spreadin' fear and gory

It's just fertilizer

For our new story

All Aboard The Glory Train

Come on now

Come on aboard

There's room for all

No need to hoard

Catch the Energy

And move on out

We can do this

Have no doubt

All aboard the Glory Train

Our life will never

Be the same

Woo Hoo

All Aboard The Glory Train

Chugga, Chugga

Boom, Boom

Flash

The ride is free

You don't need cash

Watch It change

It's our Time now

Turn around, jump down

Holy Cow

Are you up?

Are you awake?

All Aboard The Glory Train

Let's get goin'

Take off the brake

Woo Hoo

Chugga, Chugga

Boom, Boom

Flash

The Time is Now

The past is past

Walkin' Music

I got springs in my body

I got springs in my feet

I bounce when I walk

I bounce down the street

I bounce up the steps

I bounce in the house

I bounce in the church

I bounce for the mouse

I bounce in the store

I bounce in the mall

I bounce and I bounce

And I never fall

Walkin' Music

I bounce for Jekyll

I bounce for Hyde

I bounce for them all

Cause I'm happy inside

Ain't got no fear

And nothin' to hide

Springs on my feet

And rubber bands on my hands

Listen to my music

I am my own band

I dance through the day

All over the place

Walkin' Music

I'm here to champion

The whole human race

I've got rings on my fingers

And bells on my toes

When I walk down the street

Everyone knows

We Love You, America

Oh, Yeah, I know how to play the game

But really, People, it's so lame

To pretend that all is pumpkin pie

While they're spitting in your eye

It's our country, do or die

The banks were broke

We made them rich

Then they stole our homes

Now that's a bitch

We Love You, America

The Wall Street Gang

Got away with their crimes

We took the rap

And paid their fines

Come on now, it's so insane

To accept what they're doing

To Dick and Jane

It is, indeed, a dark, dark game

We Love You, America

Wake up, People,

Something's not right

When the people hurt most

Don't stand up and fight

We've had enough

It's way too much

With all the corruption,

Hidden agenda and such

We Love You, America

Our freedom's disappearing

Our kids have gone wild

Our country's goin' down

Every man, woman, child

America, America

We can change our fate

Remember from the beginning

What made this country great

We Love You, America

They raised our taxes

Way too much

Are they evil or

Just out of touch

You go on line

They see you

The Government's playing

Peek-a-Boo

We Love You, America

If the chemtrails don't get you

Then HAARP will

Or that new pharmaceutical

In the form of a pill

Is this out of ignorance

Or is it a plot?

However it is

May the power brokers rot

We Love You, America

Oops, this may not be the way

Should we love them back to health

So they can stay

And share their wealth?

Hey, Folks,

Things just aren't right

Straighten up your backbone

And join the fight

We Love You, America

America, America

It's not too late

To renew our Spirit

Our country, our fate

Come along and join us

If you're a patriot

Don't just sit there

Don't just rot

We Love You, America

Our country is transfiguring

Many are now awake

Honest leaders are ready

To run the ship of state

We don't need bad politics

We know what's right

We won't go down

Without a fierce fight

We Love You, America

We have the guts

Integrity and Spirit

Nothing can conquer us

Unless we fear it

In fact you know

We're going to win

We'll heal the decay

From deep within

We Love You, America

First thing to do

Is clean the whole house

Go after the rats

Even the mouse

We have a great country

We stand strong

We are willing to change

And correct what's wrong

We Love You, America

We love you, America

We'll do you right

God forgive us

Our oversight

The Statue of Liberty

Will again shine her Light

As we fill with gratitude

All day unto night

We Love You, America

God blessed this land

And He'll forgive

Our blindness and

The way we've lived

We'll purge ourselves

And develop our Light

God forgive us

Our oversight

We Love You, America

We'll extend our hand

To all our brothers

In our land

And in all others

America, America

We love you so

As we open our hearts

And let it flow

We Love You, America

Together we can do this

Yes, we can

America's still

Our blessed Land

Recipe for Change

The world's gone crazy, take me home

Just watching the news

Gives me post traumatic stress syndrome

I think the problem truly is

Terribly misguided testosterone

Where are the women

Who birthed these boys?

Why don't they standup

And make some noise

Recipe for Change

To keep their DNA

In check

So their offspring don't

Bully the world to heck?

By boys I mean

All men worldwide

Who abuse their power

And then try to hide

Recipe for Change

Come on, Women

Let's take on our Power

Wake Up, Wake Up

This is our Hour

The world needs

To hear our voice

We're down to the wire

And have no choice

Recipe for Change

But Life or Death

No, it's not the time

To hold

Your breath

Let's take the world back

Let it renew, and rest

And then clean up

Its dirty nest

Recipe for Change

No more war

No, not anymore

No more killing

No more gore

The world is crying

For our direction

The feminine touch

To bring correction

Recipe for Change

What happened to values

Like kindness and integrity

The Universal codes

Of worldwide decency

We can get out of the mind

And move into the heart

Teach this to the world

That's a great start

Recipe for Change

We are very capable

Of leading

With true power

No more pleading

Let's take the helm

Of leadership together

To co-create a world

Where we'd like to live forever

Recipe for Change

A world that is noble and just

Fitting for the God self

That lives within each one of us

Deep in the heart of every Human Being

Let's lift the ignorance

So all of us can be seen

For who we truly are

Magnificent Beings birthed from a star

Recipe for Change

Together we can do this

Hand in hand

No more mistreatment

Upon this Sacred Land

Mother Earth, Father Sky

Brother Sun, Great Spirit

We are ready to Listen

We are ready to hear it

Recipe for Change

We open our Hearts to You

Fill them full

With Light from Above

Help us to radiate Your Love

So we can help

Heal our world once more

One in which all Your children will flourish

Completely healed to their core

Recipe for Change

No more fear

But love instead

To grace and protect

Every family's homestead

The Golden Age

Has just begun

The Bell of True Freedom

At last has rung

OMG and GMO

GMO and OMG

What are they doin'

To you and me?

Are they makin' us

Guinea pig robots

While all our farmland

Spoils and rots?

Come on folks

Wake up, wake up

Open your eyes

Or we'll be gifted

With an ugly surprise

OMG and GMO

That's embedded deep in our bodies

For our programmed demise

OMG and GMO

They're dangerous folks

They gotta go

Let's vote with our groceries

And just say no

No, no, no

We say no

To GMO

At the Mall

What a trip

I'm at the mall

No one sees me

No one at all

I'm 4 feet wide

And 12 feet tall

Just quietly walkin'

At the mall

I'm neon electric

But calm inside

Glowing colors

Cover my hide

At the Mall

My smile is wide

From ear to ear

My mind is healed

And sparkling clear

My heart's my guide

It's my new brain

It shows me where

To park my train

No one sees me

It's so much fun

The secret's mine

My life's begun

References

Matt Kahn

Tarek Bibi

Lanna Spencer

Debora Wayne

Raquel Spencer

Andie DePass

Lottie Cooper

Christel Hughes

Sophia Zoe

Dipal Shah

Cathy Hohmeyer

Jenny Ngo

Morry Zelcovitch.

Tamra Oviatt

Lynn Waldrop

John Newton

Dorian Light

Stacey Mayo

Neale Donald Walsch

Marianne Williamson

Julie Renee

Lisa Transcendence Brown

SARK

Judy Cali

Vandana Shiva

Masanobu Fukuoka

Tulsi Gabbard

Paul Stamets

M. T. Keshe

Buckmaster Fuller

Santos Bonacci

David Wilcock

Cosmic Ordering Made Easier
by Ellen Watts

Crimes Against Nature
by Robert F. Kennedy, Jr.

The Emotion Code
by Bradley Nelson

Emotional Freedom Technique (EFT)

Ho'oponopono

YouWealthRevolution.com

FromHeartacheToJoy.com

AcousticHealth.com

GalacticConnection.com

StarKnowledgeEnterprises.com

FoodBabe.com

Bioneers.org

NextWorldTV.com

Homeopathic Cell Salts

Optimum Health Institute

birthingandrebirthing.com

NotesFromTheUniverse.com

NewPhoenixRising.com

Acim.org

Wopg.org

About the Author

After working many years in the public sector Nadja is reinventing herself as an artist and writer. She has an eclectic background. Her joys include adventuring on the Open Road, dancing, cooking, being in nature, writing and painting. She is also interested in natural building, organic gardening, alternative health, life-long learning, travel, and living moment to moment. Nadja writes for the conscious community and people who are interested in healing, meditation, transformation, ascension, and the New Earth. This includes highly sensitive people, Starseeds, Indigos, empaths, Light Workers, energy healers, artists, visionaries, and those in recovery and discovery.

Work by Nadja

Soft-cover books, eBooks, MP3s, and CDs

Smashwords, Amazon, Kindle, iBooks, CreateSpace,

CDBaby, iTunes, YouTube, and your local bookstore by

request.

River of Living Light

Evolution Revolution

Random Thoughts and Poems

Hopi Blue Corn

El Maiz Azul de los Hopis

Visionary Tales for the New Earth

Color Me Bright Coloring Book

Blue Sky

Ascension Codes

Raps, Chants, and Rants

Women's Power Awakened

Ozzengoggle Poems

From the City of Shem

You Are Not Alone

Family Secrets

Flying Heart

Bullies